To my amazing grandchildren Gavin, Skyler and Zoey

*In memory of my mother, Libby, who died at 101
and was witness to all the changes of the 20th century.
I miss you, Mom.*

Disclaimer: This is a work of fiction. Names, characters, places and incidents are either the product of the author's imagination or used fictitiously. Any resemblance to actual persons, living or dead, is entirely coincidental.

Text © 2021 Sharon Rosenblatt Kramer
Illustrations © 2021 Michael Sayre

All rights reserved. No part of this publication may be reproduced without the prior written permission of the publisher, except in the case of brief quotations embodied in critical reviews and certain other noncommercial uses permitted by copyright law. For permission requests, contact the publisher at the address below.
Golden Alley Press
37 S. Sixth Street
Emmaus, PA 18049

www.goldenalleypress.com

The text of this book is set in Times
Book designed by Michael Sayre

Printed in United States of America
1 3 5 7 9 10 8 6 4 2

Time for Bubbe / Sharon Rosenblatt Kramer

ISBN 978-1-7333055-7-0 Paperback
ISBN 978-1-7333055-8-7 eBook

Time for Bubbe

SHARON ROSENBLATT KRAMER

PICTURES BY MICHAEL SAYRE

 **Golden Alley Press**
Emmaus, Pennsylvania

Bubbe meets me in the lobby of her building.

We ride the elevator to her apartment on the 18th floor.

I press every button. The lights come on one by one.

By the time we reach the 10th floor, the elevator doors have opened and closed 10 times. What have I done?

Bubbe pats my *tuches*.

"Don't worry, my *boychik*. I have all the time in the world."

I take care of my bubbe once a week.

Bubbe is my great-grandmother. She is 96 years old. I am 6.

If she could stand up straight, which she can't because her back hurts, she would be taller than me.

Because she stoops over, we are almost the same height.

Bubbe uses a walker when she goes outside.

A walker is like a bike for old people. It has a seat for her to rest on and a basket for groceries. I wish it had a bell.

I like to pretend the walker is a train. I move it around Bubbe's apartment on make-believe tracks.

Sometimes I sit on the seat while Bubbe pushes me. We go into the kitchen, through tunnels, past the bedroom and over bridges.

"One more time?" I ask.

"I have all the time in the world, Bubbalah," Bubbe says as we go around and around.

Bubbe keeps a flyswatter in a tall blue vase by her window.

I've never seen a fly in her apartment.

"If I ever see a fly, I am ready for it," she says.

I sweep my magic-wand flyswatter over the glass birds and photographs on the coffee table.
"Abracadabra! Now you see it; now you don't!"
Everything disappears and then I bring it back.

Bubbe tells me the names of everyone in her photos.

The largest photo is Zaydee. He is not smiling and has a beard that looks like cotton candy.

There is a picture of Bubbe's mother. I am surprised to hear that Bubbe has a mother.

"My mother was born in Russia," she tells me.

"That one is my brother Hymie. He quit school and got in with a bad crowd. No *naches* for my mother from him."

Bubbe points to a picture of her brother Lou.

"A real *mensch*," she says. "He was always good to me and my family."

Bubbe loves a *nosh*.

We pack a picnic and put it in the walker's basket.

We go down to the second floor to buy M&M's from the candy machine. Then we head to the party room.

In the party room, I bang on the piano and Bubbe hums. Her walker sways in time to the music.

"Would you believe that I used to be a good dancer?" she says.

We eat our M&M's one color at a time, starting with the red ones. We lift our apple juice boxes and toast each other.

"L'chiam!" we say together.

Then we eat peanut butter and jelly sandwiches on warm *challah* bread.

There are six rows of mailboxes.

"My box is the first one in the bottom row," Bubbe tells me. "The manager gave me that box because I couldn't reach my other box without help. What *tsuris* I went through just to get my mail!"

Bubbe hands me the key. I open her box. It is empty.

"You know what this mailbox is worth?" she says. *"Bubkes."*

I decide to write Bubbe a letter when I get home so she can have some mail. She'll be surprised to hear from me.

Bubbe always wears a scarf around her neck. In a drawer in her bedroom are red ones, pink ones, long ones, short ones.

Bubbe puts a green and black scarf around my head and tells me I look like a pirate.

Next she takes a red scarf and makes a cape for me. I am a bullfighter.

Bubbe grabs her pink slippers to use as bull's horns. We face each other and circle around the room pretending to be in a fight.

"*Oy vey*," Bubbe says. "I must be *meshuga* to run around with pink slippers on my head.

Bubbalah, find my walker."

Bubbe goes back to the scarf drawer and pulls out a white scarf, puts it around my waist and ties it in the back.

"Now you are a real *kukher*," she says. "Let's make some noodle *kugel*."

Bubbe fills a large pot with water. When it boils, she places wide noodles in the pot.

My job is to crack four eggs on the edge of the bowl, mix them with a fork, and add a *bissel* of salt. I bash each egg on the edge of the bowl until the egg comes out of its shell.

Bubbe puts on her glasses to check my work.

"Mazel tov," she says. "Not one shell in the bowl."

Bubbe adds cottage cheese, sour cream, butter, sugar, raisins, and the cooked noodles.

I add cinnamon, but not too much.

"Does your mother like noodle kugel?" she asks.

"I don't know."

"Well, she'll like mine. Mine is the best. I'll send some home with you."

Bubbe pours the mixture into a baking dish. I put some slices of butter on top and sprinkle cinnamon over it all.

I think I overdo the cinnamon, but Bubbe doesn't say anything.

She winks at me and puts it in the oven.

"Good job," she says.

"Bubbe, do you have any toys?"

"I don't have toys," Bubbe says, "but I have pots and pans and bowls and spoons. When I was a girl, that's what my mother gave me for toys. Better than any of that *khazeray* they sell in the stores."

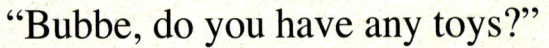

Bubbe spreads pots, pans, bowls and spoons on the kitchen floor.

I make a farm with a barn and a lake.

"Bubbe, can I put some water in the lake?"

"Just a bissel," she says.

Glossary of Yiddish Words

Yiddish word	What it means	How to say it
bissel	small amount	*biss-el*
boychik	boy or young man	*boi-chik*
bubbalah	sweetheart, loved one often used by grandparents	*bu-ba-la*
bubbe	grandmother	*bub-ee*
bubkes	of no value; worth nothing	*bub-kiss*
challah	Jewish egg bread	*hol-lah*
Hebrew	national language of Israel	*he-brew*
khazeray	junk	*khaz-er-ay*
kugel	baked pudding or cassserole usually made from egg noodles; often baked during holidays	*ku-gil*
kukher	a cook	*cook-er*
l'chaim	"to life" a toast to wish someone a good life	*la-ki-em*
meshuga	crazy, foolish	*meh-shoo-geh*
mazel tov	congratulations	*ma-zel-tov*

Yiddish word	What it means	How to say it
mensch	person who helps others	*men-tch*
naches	joy	*nakh-es*
nosh	a snack	*nosh*
oy vey	said when upset or surprised	*oye-vey*
sheyn eyngl	beautiful boy	*shay-na angle*
sheyn meydl	beautiful girl	*shay-na mey-dill*
tsuris	problems or trouble	*tsur-is*
tuches	rear end	*tah-kiss*
Yiddish	language spoken for over a thousand years by Jews in Central and Eastern Europe	*yi-dish*
zaydee	grandfather	*zade-ee*

Yiddish is a language that was spoken for nearly a thousand years by millions of Jewish people living in Central and Eastern Europe. Most Yiddish words were borrowed from German, some were from Hebrew, and the rest were from many other languages, depending on where the Jewish people lived.

A Note from the Author

My grandmother came to the United States from Russia in 1888, when she was 12 years old. She read Yiddish books and newspapers. She went to Yiddish plays. When she grew up and married, my grandmother had seven children – including my mother. They spoke Yiddish at home but spoke English when they were outside and at school.

When I was a young girl, my grandmother lived with us. She and my mother spoke Yiddish to each other. I understood many of the Yiddish words they used.

The bubbe in the story is my mother. The boy in the story is my grandson. He knows a few Yiddish words and I think he is a real mensch.

About the Author

SHARON KRAMER grew up in Chicago, but she has also lived in Los Angeles, New York, Albuquerque, and Minneapolis.

Sharon has always been a teacher of some kind, her students ranging from 3rd and 5th graders to attorneys and ex-convicts. Now retired, she keeps busy with memoir writing, photography, urban sketching, and enjoying her grandchildren.

Time for Bubbe is Sharon's first book.

Sharon welcomes comments from readers.

Contact her via email: sharon.kramer@goldenalleypress.com.

Bubbe's Recipe for the Best Noodle Kugel Ever

8 oz. package of wide, flat noodles
¼ cup (½ stick) butter, divided into 4 parts
3 large eggs
1 cup sour cream
1 cup cottage cheese
¼ cup sugar
½ tsp. vanilla extract
½ cup raisins (soak until needed)
A bissel (dash) of salt
3 tsp. cinnamon, divided
¼ cup brown sugar for top (optional)

- Preheat oven to 350 degrees.
- Butter an 8 x 8 baking dish.
- Cook noodles in lightly salted boiling water for minimum time directed on package.
- Drain noodles; rinse quickly under cold water. Add two parts of divided butter to hot noodles.
- In a separate bowl, stir together eggs, sour cream, cottage cheese, sugar, vanilla extract, raisins (drained), and salt. Add 2 tsp. of cinnamon.
- Add noodles to mixture and stir to mix.
- Pour noodle mixture into baking dish. Sprinkle top with brown sugar (optional) and remaining 1 tsp. cinnamon. Dot with remaining butter.
- Bake for 1 hour 10 minutes or until golden brown.
- Cool for 30 minutes before slicing into squares.

Thank You

*Thank you to my teacher and friend Beth Finke
for her encouragement and wisdom.*

Made in the USA
Monee, IL
08 December 2021